For Gwennie Smith, a "grammy"
who is always on the nice list

**AH**


For my Mum, who filled my childhood with
my favourite things: pencils, paper, and hugs

**AC**

 little bee books

New York, NY

Text copyright © 2022 by Alastair Heim

Illustrations copyright © 2022 by Alisa Coburn

All rights reserved, including the right of reproduction in whole or in part in any form.

Library of Congress Cataloging-in-Publication Data is available upon request.

Manufactured in China   TPL 0723

First Edition   10 9 8 7 6 5 4 3 2

ISBN 978-1-4998-1258-9

For information about special discounts on bulk purchases,

please contact Little Bee Books at sales@littlebeebooks.com.

littlebeebooks.com

# HELLO, TREE

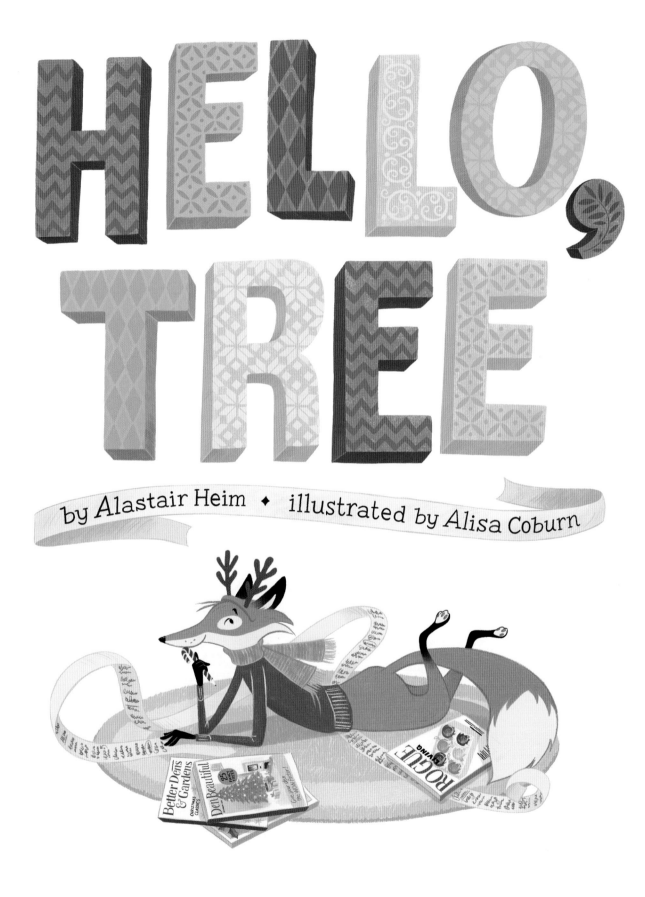

by Alastair Heim ◆ illustrated by Alisa Coburn

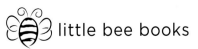
little bee books

**Hello, tree.**

CHRISTMAS TREES

WE
DELIVER

z z z

Check out
~our~
wreaths

FRESH!

PINE ........ $
SPRUCE ..... $
FIR ........... $

**Hello, twine.**

Hello, wreath.

Hello, sign.

Hello, snowman.

CRUNCH!
MUNCH!

Hello, nose.

**Hello, soldier.**

**Hello, clothes.**

Hello, cocoa.

Hello, trains.

GINGERBREAD TRAIN
GINGERBREAD TRAIN
GINGERBREAD TRAIN
GINGERBREAD TRAIN
GINGERBREAD TRAIN

**Hello, pretty candy canes.**

**Hello, bells.**

**Hello, bow.**

**Hello, flowers.**

LE FANCY PANTS CAFE

**Hello, strings.**

**HELLO, ALL YOU CHRISTMAS THINGS!!!**

**Hello, stocking.**

**Hello, hook.**

**Hello, candle.**

**Hello, book.**

Bye-bye, cookies
I just ate!

URP!

**Night-night, chimney.**

**Night-night, flue.**

**Night-night, letter.**

**Night, night . . .**

THE PARK

PÂTISSERIE MÉLANIE

CHRISTMAS TREES

FOXY'S DEN

**Hello, morning.**

# Hello, TREE!